Engine Nine, Feelin' Fine!

By Bill Scollon
Based on an episode by Chris Nee
Based on the series created by Chris Nee
Illustrated by Character Building Studio
and the Disney Storybook Artists

DISNEY PRESS
New York

SUSTAINABLE FORESTRY INITIATIVE
Certified Chain of Custody
Promoting Sustainable Forestry
www.sfiprogram.org
SFI-01415
The SFI label applies to the text stock

"Lambie!" calls Doc McStuffins. "It's time to open the clinic."
Doc can't find Lambie anywhere. "Has anyone seen Lambie?" she asks.
"Oops!" Doc giggles. She puts on her magic stethoscope and her toys spring to life.
"I don't know where she is!" Stuffy says.

Suddenly, Doc's brother bursts into her room, pushing his toy fire engine.
In a flash, Doc's toys go stuffed!
"Will you play firefighter with me?" Donny asks.
"Maybe later, okay?" says Doc.
Doc scoops up Lambie and Stuffy as Donny leaves.

Doc hurries out to the backyard.

"I'm going outside to play, Mom!" she calls.

"Okay, sweetie," Doc's mom says. "Just take care. It's a very hot day!"

"I will," Doc answers.

Doc McStuffins opens the door to her clinic and flips over the welcome sign. "The Doc is in!" she says.

"Hi, Hallie!" says Doc. "Do we have any toys that need fixing?"
"No patients yet," answers Hallie. "My, my. It sure is hot today."
"It's even too hot to cuddle," says Lambie.

Just then, Squeakers bounces through the door.

"Squeak, squeak, squeeeeaaak!"

"What's he saying?" Stuffy asks.

"I don't know. I don't speak squeak," says Hallie.

Doc has an idea. "Squeakers, can you *show* us what's wrong?"

Squeakers leads Doc and the others into the backyard.

"What's wrong with you, Engine Nine?" says Donny. "I'll give you one more chance, but that's it." He pumps Lenny's siren and points Lenny's hose at a pretend fire, but nothing comes out! "Oh no," says Donny. "You're broken!"

Donny sets Lenny on a pile of broken toys.

"Sorry, Lenny," he says sadly. "You were an awesome toy. I'm going to miss you."

"Awww, Donny looks so sad," says Doc.

"I know how you can cheer up Donny," says Lambie.

"Fix Lenny!" Stuffy says.

As soon as Donny walks away, Doc and the others run over to Lenny. "What's wrong, Lenny?" asks Stuffy.

"I keep running out of water," Lenny says. "A fire truck that can't put out a fire isn't much good."

"Let's get you to the clinic, Lenny," Doc says. "It's time for a checkup."

Lenny is a little nervous. "What is a checkup, anyway?" he asks.
"It's when a doctor takes a look at you to make sure you're healthy," says Lambie.
Doc listens to Lenny's heartbeat.

"Sounds perfect," she says. "Lenny, has anything been bothering you?"
"Well, I've been feeling kind of tired and my head hurts sometimes," Lenny admits.
"Mostly on really hot days."

15

Just then, there's a knock at the door!
"Doc, I have something for you!" calls Doc's mom.
"Hurry," Doc says to her toys. "Go stuffed!"

"Hi, Mom," says Doc. "What's up?"

"I brought you some water, sweetie," says Doc's mom. "I don't want you to get dehydrated."

"What's dehydrated?" Doc asks.

"If you don't drink enough water, especially on a hot day, you can feel sick."

"Dehydrated," repeats Doc. "That's it! Thanks, Mom."

"I know what's wrong," announces Doc. "Lenny, you have Driedout-a-tosis!"
"Oh, my! That sounds like it should go straight into the Big Book of Boo-Boos!"
says Hallie.

"What's Driedout-a-tosis mean, Doc?" asks Lenny.
"It's like when you are dehydrated. Dehydrated is when you aren't drinking enough water," Doc explains. "Drinking water is important. But when it's hot outside, it's even *more* important!"

Doc puts the glass of water in front of Lenny. "Drink it all up," she says.
"Ah," says Lenny. "I feel better already!"

Hallie looks into the fire hose. "Is this thing working now?" she asks.
Squirt! "Yep, it sure as stuffin' is!" laughs Hallie.

Donny is surprised to see Doc with his fire truck. "Engine Nine!
What are you doing here?"
Lenny shoots a stream of water out of his hose.
"Awesome!" Donny shouts. "You're working again! I missed you, buddy."

"Help! Help!" shouts Doc. "We have to rescue Stuffy from the burning building!"
"Don't worry, Stuffy," yells Donny. "Engine Nine will save you!"

22

Donny points Lenny's hose at the pretend fire and water gushes out!
"Whoa!" Donny says. "Great job, Engine Nine!"

"Thanks for playing with me, Doc," Donny says. "You're the best sister ever."
"I love hanging out with you, Donny," says Doc. "Almost as much as our toys do!"